BIOGRAPHIES

Martha Washington

First Lady of the United States

by SUZANNE SLADE illustrated by FRANCES MOORE

PICTURE WINDOW BOOKS
Minneapolis, Minnesota

Special thanks to our advisers for their expertise:

Melissa J. Doak, Ph.D., Independent writer
WriteOn Writing Services
Ithaca, New York

Terry Flaherty, Ph.D., Professor of English
Minnesota State University, Mankato

Editors: Jill Kalz and Shelly Lyons
Designer: Nathan Gassman
Page Production: Michelle Biedscheid
Associate Managing Editor: Christianne Jones
The illustrations in this book were created digitally.
Photo Credit: Library of Congress, page 3

Picture Window Books
151 Good Counsel Drive
P.O. Box 669
Mankato, MN 56002-0669
877-845-8392
www.picturewindowbooks.com

Printed in the United States of America.

All books published by Picture Window Books are manufactured with paper containing at least 10 percent post-consumer waste.

Library of Congress Cataloging-in-Publication Data
Slade, Suzanne.
Martha Washington : first lady of the United States / by Suzanne Slade ; illustrated by Frances Moore.
p. cm. — (Biographies)
ISBN-13: 978-1-4048-3727-0 (library binding)
1. Washington, Martha, 1731-1802—Juvenile literature. 2. Presidents' spouses—United States—Biography—Juvenile literature. I. Moore, Frances. II. Title.
E312.19.W34S58 2008
973.4'1092—dc22
[B] 2007004286

Martha Washington is best known as the wife of George Washington, the first president of the United States. Martha was a loving wife and mother. She spent most of her time caring for her family, but she also visited sick and lonely soldiers in Army camps during the Revolutionary War (1775–1783).

People today still remember the kindness and strength of the first woman to become the first lady of the United States.

This is the story of

Martha Washington.

Martha Dandridge was born in 1731 on Chestnut Grove plantation. She was the first of John and Frances Dandridge's nine children. John was a tobacco grower.

When Martha was young, America was made up of 13 Colonies. The Colonies were ruled by Great Britain. Martha was born in Virginia.

Martha enjoyed taking care of her younger brothers and sisters. Her mother taught her to read and write. Her mother also taught her the manners of a young lady and how to cook and sew. In her free time, Martha loved to ride horses. She was a very skilled rider.

Growing up, Martha became friends with a kind neighbor named Daniel Custis. Daniel came from a family that had a lot of money.

When Martha turned 17, Daniel began coming to her house often to visit. They fell in love and were married in 1750. The wedding was held in Martha's home.

Martha and her husband lived near Chestnut Grove. They moved into a large two-story house on the Pamunkey River. Their first child, Daniel Parke Custis, was born in 1751. They later had three more children named Frances, John, and Martha. Everyone called John "Jacky" and young Martha "Patsy."

Martha's husband ran the Custis plantation and owned hundreds of slaves. Martha was in charge of the house slaves and the children's nursemaids.

Martha and her husband lived well and shared much happiness, but they also faced sad times. Their firstborn son, Daniel, died in 1754, at the age of 3. In 1757, their daughter Frances died. Later that same year, Martha's husband also became ill and died. With two young children to raise, Martha became a widow at the age of 26.

Custis
757

Nine months later, a man named George Washington stopped at Martha's home. Colonel Washington was heading to Williamsburg on a business trip. George was kind and smart. He was also a fine horseman.

Martha asked George to stay for dinner. Within a few weeks, he asked Martha to be his wife. They were married in 1759. Soon after, the Washington family moved to Mount Vernon, George's family plantation in Virginia.

From 1775 to 1783, George led the American Army as it fought against the British for freedom. This fight was called the Revolutionary War. Martha traveled to every winter Army camp to stay with George. While there, she worked hard to raise the soldiers' spirits. She talked with visiting officials. She also raised money to buy supplies for the Army.

In 1789, George was named the first president of the United States. The Washingtons lived in New York City and Philadelphia, Pennsylvania, during the years George served as president.

The president's wife is known as the first lady. Martha was the first lady of the United States for eight years. She often held large dinner parties. Many people wanted to visit the president and share their problems and ideas with him.

Martha and George did not have much time alone. After Martha's son Jacky died during the Revolutionary War, Martha and George spent their days raising two of Jacky's four children, "Wash" and "Nelly." They also spent time helping the United States become a strong country.

In 1797, the second president of the United States, John Adams, took office. Martha and George moved back to Mount Vernon. They enjoyed two peaceful years together before George died in 1799.

Although Martha missed George deeply, she was not alone. Her grandchildren Wash and Nelly lived with her at Mount Vernon. Nelly's husband, Lawrence, and their two children stayed there, too.

In 1802, Martha Washington died at the age of 70 in her home. Her body was buried at Mount Vernon beside her husband, George.

The Life of Martha Washington

1731	Born June 2 on a plantation near Williamsburg, Virginia
1750	Married Daniel Parke Custis
1751	Gave birth to her first child, Daniel
1753	Had her daughter Frances
1754	Gave birth to John; son Daniel died
1756	Had her last child, Martha
1757	Daughter Frances died; became a widow when Daniel Custis died
1759	Married George Washington and moved to Mount Vernon
1773	Daughter Patsy died
1781	Son Jacky died
1789–1797	Served as first lady of the United States
1802	Died at her home in Mount Vernon on May 22

Did You Know?

- Martha's daughter Patsy suffered from an illness called epilepsy. She died in 1773, when she was just 17 years old.
- After Jacky's death, Martha and George adopted two of their grandchildren. The children's mother, Nelly, had four children and was expecting another baby. Nelly decided it would be a good idea for two children to move to Mount Vernon. It was common during this time for people to adopt children within their family.
- Martha was more than 12 inches (30.5 centimeters) shorter than George Washington. He was 6 feet 2½ inches (189.2 cm) tall.
- Martha always tried to look her best while serving as first lady. She put white powder on her hair, as did most people in the 1700s. She also wore a long dress every day.
- George and Martha were the only president and first lady who never lived in the White House. Workers started building the White House in 1792. It was finished in 1800, three years after George left the office of president.
- A year before she died, Martha burned hundreds of letters she and George had written to each other while they were apart. Martha didn't want other people to read her love letters.

Glossary

Colonies — the 13 groups of people living in North America before the Revolutionary War; they were ruled by Great Britain

nursemaids — women whose jobs are to look after children

plantation — a large farm where crops are grown

Revolutionary War — (1775–1783) the Colonies' fight for freedom from Great Britain; the Colonies later became the United States of America

slaves — people who are owned by other people

tobacco — a plant that is dried and smoked by people

widow — a woman whose husband has died

To Learn More

At the Library

Ashby, Ruth. *George and Martha Washington.* Milwaukee: World Almanac Library, 2005.

Ransom, Candice. *Martha Washington.* Minneapolis: Carolrhoda Books, 2003.

Simon, Charnan. *Martha Dandridge Custis Washington.* New York: Children's Press, 2000.

On the Web

FactHound offers a safe, fun way to find Web sites related to this book. All of the sites on FactHound have been researched by our staff.

1. Visit *www.facthound.com*
2. Type in this special code: 1404837272
3. Click on the FETCH IT button.

Your trusty FactHound will fetch the best sites for you!

Index

Look for all of the books in the Biographies series:

Abraham Lincoln: *Lawyer, President, Emancipator*

Albert Einstein: *Scientist and Genius*

Amelia Earhart: *Female Pioneer in Flight*

Benjamin Franklin: *Writer, Inventor, Statesman*

Cesar Chavez: *Champion and Voice of Farmworkers*

Frederick Douglass: *Writer, Speaker, and Opponent of Slavery*

George Washington: *Farmer, Soldier, President*

George Washington Carver: *Teacher, Scientist, and Inventor*

Harriet Tubman: *Hero of the Underground Railroad*

Martha Washington: *First Lady of the United States*

Martin Luther King Jr.: *Preacher, Freedom Fighter, Peacemaker*

Pocahontas: *Peacemaker and Friend to the Colonists*

Sally Ride: *Astronaut, Scientist, Teacher*

Sojourner Truth: *Preacher for Freedom and Equality*

Susan B. Anthony: *Fighter for Freedom and Equality*

Thomas Edison: *Inventor, Scientist, and Genius*